P9-CEP-497

EASY   C 36220
FICTION

Quackenbush, Robert
    Henry's Awful Mistake.

BEECHER ROAD SCHOOL LIBRARY
WOODBRIDGE, CT 06525

DEMCO

Beecher Road School Library

3 6 2 2 0

HENRY'S AWFUL MISTAKE

by Robert Quackenbush

PARENTS MAGAZINE PRESS · NEW YORK

A Parents Magazine
Read Aloud Original.

Copyright © 1980 by Robert Quackenbush.
All rights reserved.
Printed in the United States of America.
12 13 14 15 16 17 18 19 20

Library of Congress Cataloging in Publication Data
Quackenbush, Robert M.   Henry's awful mistake.
SUMMARY: Henry the duck tries all sorts of methods to rid
his kitchen of an ant before his guest comes to supper.
[1. Humorous stories.   2. Ducks — Fiction.
3. Ants — Fiction]   I. Title
PZ7.Q16He   [E]   80 – 20327
ISBN 0 – 8193 – 1039 – 5   ISBN 0 – 8193 - 1040 – 9 lib bdg.

For Piet
and his Grandma Q.
and Margie
and Leslie B.

The day Henry the Duck
asked his friend Clara
over for supper,
he found an ant
in the kitchen.

Henry was worried
that Clara
would see the ant.
She might think
his house was not clean.
The ant had to go.

Henry reached for
a can of ant spray.
But he didn't want
to spray near the food
he was cooking.
So he chased the ant
with a frying pan.

Henry ran around
the kitchen,
chasing after the ant.
But the ant got away
and hid behind the stove.

Henry took the food
he was cooking
off the stove.
Then he shut off the flame
and pulled the stove
away from the wall.
He saw the ant!

The ant saw Henry
and ran into
a small crack in the wall.
Henry went and got
a hammer.

Henry pounded a big
hole in the wall
where the crack was.
But he couldn't find the ant.
So he kept on pounding.

The hole got bigger
and bigger.
At last, Henry saw
the ant sitting
on a pipe inside
the wall.

Henry aimed the hammer
at the ant—and missed.
The blow of the hammer
broke the pipe.

Water came shooting
out of the pipe.
Henry couldn't stop it.

Henry grabbed a towel.
He tied it around the pipe
and the water stopped
shooting out.

But Henry hadn't stopped
the water soon enough.
It had sprayed
all over the kitchen.
Everything was soaking wet,
except for Clara's supper,
thank goodness.

Henry began mopping up
the puddles of water.
All at once, he slipped and
banged against the
kitchen table.
Everything came
crashing down.
Henry was covered with
pots and pans and food.

The supper was ruined.
There was nothing
Henry could do now
but to call Clara
and tell her not to come.

While Henry was
talking on the telephone,
the towel came loose
from the pipe.
The water came shooting out
and flooded the whole house.
Henry was carried right out
the front door by the flood.

There was no going back.
Poor Henry's house was
washed away by the flood.
He saved what he could
and moved into
a new house.

When Henry was settled
in his new house,
he again asked Clara
over for supper.
Just as he went to the door
to let Clara in,
he saw an ant.

He looked the other way!

ABOUT THE AUTHOR

Some time ago, ROBERT QUACKENBUSH received a letter from a young reader who was puzzled by his name. "Are you really a duck?" the letter writer asked. Mr. Quackenbush decided right then and there to write stories about a disaster-prone duck named Henry. The first, *Too Many Lollipops,* was originally published by Parents. *Henry's Awful Mistake* is the latest tale of Henry's mishaps and how he deals with them.

Robert Quackenbush is the author/illustrator of more than 40 other books and the illustrator of another 70. His artwork has been exhibited in leading museums across the U.S. and is now on display in the gallery he owns and runs in New York City. He also teaches painting, writing, and illustrating to adults and art to children there. Mr. Quackenbush lives in New York City with his wife, Margery, and their young son, Piet.

Do you know a 6–13 year old who would like to receive free information on a unique club which offers a wide selection of models to assemble, including airplanes, military vehicles, drag racers, helicopters, vans, and more?

To receive free information on this exciting club and to find out how to receive a free model kit, please write:

FREE MODEL
Dept. 83Z03
P.O. Box 10265
Des Moines, IA 50336

Offer available in the U.S. only.